Forbidden Sparks

Beverly Bergnaum

Contents

1. Chapter 1 — 1

2. Chapter 2 — 9

3. Chapter 3 — 17

4. Chapter 4 — 22

5. Chapter 5 — 28

6. Chapter 6 — 35

7. Chapter 7 — 40

8. Chapter 8 — 46

9. Chapter 9 — 54

10. Chapter 10 — 60

11. Chapter 11 — 66

12. Chapter 12 — 70

13. Chapter 13 — 74

14. Chapter 14   80

15. Chapter 15   84

16. Chapter 16   89

17. Chapter 17   93

18. Chapter 18   99

19. Chapter 19   104

20. Epilogue   109

Chapter 1

Do you feel like time passes away way too quickly doing something you love to do and Ella was doing that same thing which she loves any idea on what that will be..?

"Ella Charlotte Clark get the hell up or you will be late for your First day at the University" Evan shouted at Ella

Yes if you guessed she was sleeping you were Right!

"Mmmm" Ella moaned in her sleepShe just want her brother to stop their rant so she can peacefully sleep..

Just then the door barged open and there comes his brother still shouting.

"Ella get up or we both will be late". Evan shook her from her sleep.

Ella can't refuse his brothers soft request so she finally get up with a lot of efforts.

"Good morning Ella" Evan said and kissed ella's forehead .Ella wished him and kissed his cheeks and got of the bed standing and streching her hands.

"Get up and get ready we both can't get late" He said And walked off her room

And at that time ella's over thinking side came up and she started to think things like, will she be able to face new people, will everyone accept her, and what all things. She just shook her head and went towards her bathroom to do her daily routine .After her daily routine she went towards her closet and starts to choose her attire for her first day.And again she was confused what to wear and at that particular time two angels came to help her or let's just say barged in.

"First day of university ella woo ooh" Zoe shouted

And at that particular time Kate smacked on her head and said"Will you please be a little quite, we don't want to end up in a Otolaryngology cabin" She half screamed at Zoe.

And again Kate and Zoe starts to bicker with each other.. Sometimes ella thinks how come she the quiet introverted girl is friends with them . But still she loves them both very much and just can't live without them . They stood with her every minutes of those months when she was at her lowest .. They both love her too and they are one of those few people who heard ella screamed and laugh whole heartedly.

"Will you guys for the sake of Netflix stop it" and at the mention of Netflix they both became so silent as they were not shouting like an idiot a few seconds ago.

"Can you both help me choose an outfit for my first day please" Ella said

"You could've mentioned it earlier. You know we are always there for you and we both are literally fashion expert so yeah we both will choose the dress for you" Zoe said

"Without giving this long ass speech can you please choose for me what to wear" Ella said while going to sit in the bed ..

They both went towards her small closet and started to find her an outfit to wear on her first day.

They both after whole lot of 15 minutes choosed a White bodycon dress with a oversized denim jacket.

They asked Ella to wear it . Ella literally didn't liked that outfit much but she knows its waste to argue about them on this.

So she silently went towards her bathroom and started to get ready. She did her makeup minimal with a little touch of mascara and her favourite shea butter lipbalm.

When she came out both of her friends whistled at her she just thanked them and all three went down to the dining room from where delicious smell of bacon was coming and there Evan was cooking bacon and eggs for her dear sister ..

Ella knew he was multi tasker and he was giving them a very good example of his multi talking as he is smooching his girlfriends face while cooking breakfast .

All three girls face got heated up after seeing that. Ella just cleared her throat to grab attention and that's when they broke their breakfast session.

And at that time Both Evan and Olivia look at the floor as if it was the most interesting thing in the world.

Girls just laughed and wished her good morning. Olivia reciprocated .

As they all were eating breakfast Olivia asked"So El excited for the new day at a new university " she asked with a sweet smile.

Ella just nodded and smiled at her and all completed their breakfast in a comfortable silence.

As they kept the dishes in dishwasher Evan asked Ella to go sit in the car as he will drop her to university .

And Zoe and kate objected.

"Evan you can't do this to us . You've literally dropped her to high school every single day and now when she is finally in university . You are saying you will drop her. Is she a kid huh? We can take care of her ok . You can go in your car with oliie . We will take Ella with us in my car" Zoe said

And quickly evan objected"No! I will drop ella of to university . I can't leave her alone . If you both want to go with her for the first day at the university you both can come with us but I will drop her". Evan said

"Evan I will be fine and I really want to go with them. Please just let me live like a normal girl. I know you love me more than anything but . Please Ev please" Ella said with a sad face

Evan just heaved a sigh and Said"OK fine but once you will reach university. You will call me ok?" Evan said

"Ev we basically study at the same university" Kate said almost in a bored tone

"I know genius!! Just I will feel relieved that way so please call and I study at the dorm next to yours for your information." he said as he looked at ella with puppy dog eyes.

Ella just laughed and nodded and all three girls walked to sat in Zoe's car.

As they sat in the car . They started to talked about various things and suddenly Kate spoke.

"I want to start my first day of a new life with a cup of Lilly's Cafe latte babes" Kate said

Ella and Zoe laughed but Ella said,

"Girl what if we get late to university" Ella said

"We still have 1 hour till classes to start" Zoe defended

So, I just shrugged and at that time they both shouted And went towards the way of Sweet Eats .

Sweet eats was always that Cafe where this three went at the weird times of day they literally love their drinks and can drink those in any time at the day. Whenever they are sad they lit up their mood by coming here. If its a happy moment or a sad one they live it there itself. That Cafe was a very important part of their life. Well let just say they were quiet a big fan of caffeine .

As they enter the smell of Coffee hit their nose and they all smiled and went towards towards to place their order.Lilly looked at them smiled and said,

"Good morning girls. Happy first day at University. What can I get you all today?" She asked them.

They all ordered their usuals and waited for Lilly to prepare their drinks as she gave them their drink and at that time Ella received a call which was from her mom. She just took her drink in one hand and excused herself to go out to talk.

She received the call and was answered by a very sweet voice of her mom.

"Hey sweetie . First day huh! Rock it " she said

And they started to talk .. They shared some important things and what's going on in their lives. She even said she and ella's father will visit them soon. Ella loved her mom was coming and after a good talk of 20 minutes. She disconnected the call. And started to walk towards Cafe..

As she was walking she started to check her messages and was drinking her coffee But, suddenly she was clashed with a wall.

She thought what was a wall doing in middle of the street . And as she lifted her head to looked up at what she clashed at she was met with a muscular chest with a white T -Shirt which was now completely soaked with her hot coffee.

She panicked as started to rant "I am so so sorry! I was not looking and I bumped into you. I literally didn't mean it, I am so sorry . Don't be angry at me please. " She said while cleaning his shirt with her napkin.

She just frowned that why their no reply was coming and when she looked up she met with the most beautiful grey eyes she ever saw. And there he was an handsome adonis staring at her which a weird emotion in his eyes. They were standing in such a close proximity that he could even see golden pecks in it.

And now when he was broke out of her trance, And just beautifully smiled at her and said in his husky voice

"Its fine princess!!" He said

Ella was firstly shocked as to why such a handsome boy was smiling and talking to her when she literally gave him a bath in coffee. So she said

"Is it really fine?" She asked

He just nodded and gave him one of his charming smile . From which she flushed. Ok anyone would have he was so charming.

As he was about to ask her name she just smiled sweetly , nodded at him and starts to walk towards their car. Where they're friends would be waiting for her.

As she was walking towards their car, That stranger guy caught her wrist and asked"Whats your name?"

She was confused as to why he was asking him such a question but she really didn't want to be rude to him as she spilled all his coffee on him.

So she just replied " Ella"

Smiled and walked towards her friends. She saw both of them waiting for her and they asked what got her so long she just said her mom called leaving the meeting the adonis part.They sat in Zoe's car and started to drive towards Unive rsity.Which will lead her to her new life.

But in the back of her mind she had a feeling that , that handsome adonis will be part of her new life too and they would be meeting way more often than needed.

Chapter 2

Xavier

I never really made much friends as i am a very closed of person . And never really much people approached me because my glare was enough to scare them away . But now i am regretting why I agreed to be friends with these two bastards . My best friends.

They literally fight like children's . Both doesn't have one penny sense in them and you know they just fight over those topic which literally make me punch them in their guts. This time they are fighting where to drink coffee.

Like are they mad or what! Who fights over drinking some stupid coffee. But since last 1 hour they both are fighting over a stupid debate on where we will drink coffee today and i was just going through my phone because I was literally the least interested person in this debate.

Christian wants to drink coffee at some Sweet Eats and Aidan at Starbucks.. I was just waiting for them to decide .

"We will drink coffee at lilly's matter finished let's go" Christian said

"No we wil drink coffee at Starbucks and that's final you perv" Aidan said

"Huh you only want to drink coffee their because all the hot waitresses at the Starbucks gawk at us like we are a piece of meat" Chris scoffed .

"Like you don't enjoy it" Aidan said with a smirk.

"We are not discussing that asshole". Christian said And threw a cushion at Aidan who was laughing .

And again they started to bicker.. like sometimes i really think they bicker like girls. Even girls speak less than they both too.

"Okay!!!lets go to lillys for now and while returning from our day from University which we all three will rock by the way of course I will treat you with Starbucks cafe" Chris said

Aidan huffed and said Fine.

Fucking finally there discussion was over and we can finally go to a cafe to drink coffee and then head towards our first day at University. I really didn't want to go to university because at the end of the day I need to handle my father multi-billion dollar company then why wasting three years in a stupid university but my mom and dad always had a dream that I could also graduate from same university as them. And i literally can't say no to my parents .

So, now I am trailing out of my mansion , Aidan and chris on my tail and we left my mansion. We went towards my Lamborghini and roared of towards sweet eats.

I never really went to this sweet eats bakery but I tasted their coffees and cakes as chris is a big fan of them. And let me tell me tell not being a sweet lover and still liking their delicacies are a big thing for me.

As I was driving Aidan jumped and turned on the Radio.

Kid I am telling you.

And suddenly 'Perfect ' by Ed sheeran blasted from the radio.

"Guys do you guys really think that there is something called love at first sight ?" Aidan questioned

"Yes its there and it happens" Chris Said.

"That's just bullshit! There is nothing called this what you call love at first sight. How can a person love somebody without even knowing them huh? It's just an attraction which will fade off with time. And for the sake of God there is nothing called Love at first sight idiots" I said as I turned the radio off.

Chris just shrugged at my speech and said "Maybe you don't believe in love at first sight for now , but my heart says there will be a day when you will meet a girl accidentally who will change the way you think about life and love. When you will meet her you will feel like world faded away, like you and her are the only things left in this universe , like she is the most beautiful and precious thing you own and at that particular time you will want her to make her yours and at that sudden moment you will realise you got a love at first sight " chris said

" what are you a love guru! " I asked

"No but I am a believer at love and if you keep saying bad thing about the pure relationship of love I will curse you" he said with amusement dancing in his voice accompanied with Aidans laughter.

"Okay go on and curse me" I said And laughed

"OK you asked for it! I curse you that before the clock strikes midnight today you will have a love at first sight " he said with a poignant voice And bursted out laughing .

Me and Aidan accompanied him in laughing and we all laughed for about 5 mins. After controlling our laughter I said.

"Okay!!! Thank you for your curse Mr. Love guru" I said between laughs .

We reached Sweet Eats . It's a simple Sweet Cafe with delicious delicacies. When we entered we were hit by a strong smell of Coffee. Huh! Refreshed.

When we were walking towards counter to place our order all eyes were on us. Some eyes were looking at as seductively , some with confusion but mostly were wide with realisation. I just love When people give me attention so I just smirked and walked towards the counter .

There was a girl at the counter who by seeing us pulled her shirt a little down displaying her fake boobs. I mean why can't they behave properly with customer .

And at the same timing a timid , old lady enter the counter and started scolding that female waitresses

"I don't pay you to give seductive looks to our customers. Your behaviour is not very nice towards young customers. Next time you do this you will be out understand " she half screamed at that girl

I thought that lady will cry but she just flip her hair and walked towards a door in the backside

"Bitch" Lilly muttered under her breath.

Me, Aidan and chris looked at her with amusement dancing in our eyes. And when she looked towards us first she was confident and then she asked us

"What" She said With confusion .

"Lilly I thought you don't curse huh?" Chris said

She just laughed and we joined her too

"What you guys wanna order today" she asked

"Three mocha for us" I said

"Wait for 5 minutes please" she said And asked some waiter to prepare our drinks

We were talking of things of here and there when Lilly said our drinks our ready. We paid for it and went out of the Cafe.

We were not those type of people who likes to sit in the Cafe to finish their drinks. So we just started to talk and walk in the sidewalk.

Suddenly, Aidan received a call and he excused himself and went to attend the call.

And me and chris were talking when chris excused himself to go to buy some cookies because he was really craving some.

Now I was alone and I was walking peacefully . When suddenly a petite figure bumped with my chest which resulted her coffee to fall up in my t-shirt.

And I was just seeing my chest and think who the hell is this clumsy person doesn't they have any sense to see and walk .

And I was about to shout at her my eyes locked with the most beautiful face I ever saw. I was Awestruck like how can somebody be so beautiful. It was like all the surroundings fading away and we both were the only person left in this entire world . She was the epitome of beauty . She didn't realized I was gawking at her because she was busy trying to clean my t-shirt and ranting how sorry she was.

Today morning we discussed what would happen if somebody have a love at first sight and I very confidently admitted I will never fall in the trap of love at first.

And here despite being one of the most coldest people in the world I was staring at this beauty standing in front of me like an idiot.

Then suddenly I was greeted with those eyes directly looking at me and at that time I felt exposed like how can somebody be so beautiful. And I just had a glimpse of all my life with her. And i realised I suffered with the disease called love at first sight

I don't want her to see panicked so I said it's ok. She looked shocked but then she give one beautiful smile of hers which literally made me fall for her once again .

And she asked really . Oh my God she has a such a honey sweet voice.

I just nodded because I can't speak anymore. She just nodded, smiled and started to walk off. I can't just let her walk off without knowing her name atleast.

So, i just grabbed her wrist and she turned around confused with eyebrows frowned

"Whats your name" I asked

She looked confused at first. Any one would be as why a guy is talking to her when she soaked him in her coffee

But she hesitantly Smiled and said "Ella"

Wow! I just thought beautiful name for a beautiful girl.

She pulled her wrist from my hold and walked off and I was just like . Wow how can somebody be so perfect. And She is all mine. Period

Damn I am already gone for her .. like totally off the trails.

And at that time I made up in my mind that I will make her mine . U want to protect from all harm and ranger in real world. Be her shield, her support, her shrine , her home so wherever she goes she head back towards me.

"What are you looking at?" A voice came from my back.

I turned around and saw my two best friends lifting their eyebrows looking at me and my next line shocked them to core

"You have a good mouth , your curse worked , I think I just fell for a girl at love at first sight " I said my voice full of disbelief.

"You What?" They both Shouted in Unison.

Chapter 3

Xavier

Sometimes it feels like world stopped right? No of course not , I've not fallen in love again but the world seems to stopped for my two idiot best friends. Since I told then I've just met a girl for whom I fell . They both paused like an old tape. Not moving an inch . Was it so unbelievable for me to get a love interest. Apparently Yes, because I was the one who would give lectures how love is waste of time, how I wanted to puke when I see two people so in love. And here I was the first one in our group to fall in love. Wow

It unbearable to see their idiot faces making No expressions so I broke the chain of silence .

"Guys" I shouted

They both broke of the trance , looked here and there like they've just woken up from a deep sleep . And I was standing by the support of the sidewalk wall looking at them with a bored expression. Because literally They were over reacting

And suddenly they both looked at me wide eyed and shouted in unison making my ears go deaf

"You What?" Idiots shouted

They are idiots I am telling you

"I have fallen in love and I want that girl to be mine. Simple" I explained

"So, you the almighty Xavier Knight. Who said love was a waste of time and was stupidly debating this morning how love at first in a stupid thing now fallen in love. Just Amazing" Chris said

"You've really fallen in love huh? First I just don't want to react like this idiot . So can you please tell me the whole story that what on earth happened in one hour that your ideology on love changed" Aidan said

And so Aidan words had a logic I started to explain them what happened?

"So after you both excused yourselves, I was walking down the pavement silently drinking my coffee when suddenly a petite figure collided with my body making all her coffee fell in my shirt. I was so angry at this clumsy person on how their clumsiness ruined my t-shirt. So i was about to give on of my famous glare and a hardcore shaking speech , I was greeted by the most beautiful face I have ever saw. Her feature were so delicate like god took way too long to make her. Her nose, her rosy lips, her cheeks and the most beautiful thing in her face her beautiful brown eyes all were extravagant beautiful. I was so mesmerized with het beauty that I didn't even realised she was trying to clean up my shirt with napkin and she was apologizing again and again. Then suddenly she stopped and looked me in the eye and I was broken out of my trance . I said it's fine and she nodded and was going off but just then I caught her wrist and asked her name and she told her name was Ella" I said

But there was no expression in their faces and I suddenly remembered one important point

"And you guys will think that's just an infatuation but all those thing that Chris mentioned in morning about Love at first sight came true . " I said with dreamy eyes.

"You've really fallen in love bro" they both said amused while they shook their heads

I just gave them one of my infamous glare but again it was long gone with their one question

"If you want to make her yours . We need to find her . what's her name actually surname?" Chris asked

And here as a fool I am I don't know her surname .

"I don't know her surname" I replied

They both looked at me like I've grown horns on my head and gave me looks full of disbelief.

"Wow just wow you've finally fallen in love with someone and now you are telling me that you don't even know her surname.

Have you gone freaking nuts. Now how we will find her " Aidan said

" she was in a hurry so she didn't said her full name but by hook or by crook I will find her." I stated.

And when I looked at Aidan and chris they both just mouthed 'Whipped'.

And I just rolled my eyes and we all went towards my car to sit and go for the first day at university.

On the whole ride while driving I was thinking about Ella. How she was so perfect. And all those things. Aidan and chris were talking but I was not really in a mood to talk with anybody I just wanted to dream about ella my ella. So that's what I was doing.

As we reached university I parked the car in the VIP section because my father is a trusty of this University.

As we all three get off the car the whole area went silent all were gawking at us . Girls giving us seductive looks, some boys with shock . But there was something common in everyone's eyes that was fear.

And I just love When people are feared by me. Only those people whom I care and love are free to speak to me other than them no body means no body can breathe air within my 6 feet reach. Today one more person added to my list of favorite people.

As I started to walk off. I was about to enter the Administrative office when my eyes got locked up with a brunettes head.

Well that head seems familiar. I just shrugged and went towards the Administrative office to get required things.

As I entered the teacher there stood up and asked my name and all and gave me time table and all those shits for which i don't give two shits.

As I walked off the office I saw something or rather some

"Ella" a whisper left my lips along with two gasps of my friends and there she was my ella standing and talking to two girls . Smiling and laughing at the things they were saying.

I was so shocked that ella also study in the same university. I mean destiny played its game. I just smirked and my mind said to me

Stars are finally lined up Xavier!

Chapter 4

E^{lla}

I was always that type of person if thinking about something, I will think about it only but after seeing that handsome adonis staring into me, I was feeling like he stared right into my soul. I just can't forget how those beautiful black eyes looked in my dull brown ones.

I just shook my head and reminded myself, why am I thinking about him , it's not like we will meet again. But I somewhere in back of my mind I had a feeling I am going to see him again.

As walking and thinking about the handsome adonis , I didn't realized i reached where zoe's car was parked and both of my friends were glaring at me . When I looked at them they said very sweetly.

"Where the fuck you were ella? We've been waiting here for 20 minutes " Kate shouted at me .

I just covered my ears and shouted Let me explain.

"I got a call from my mom , I talked with her for a while . Then I....." and then I lied..... yes people I lied

"I found some really cute puppies and I started to play with them and got late" I said

"OMG girl how can you be so stupid. You got late because you were playing g with puppies. How stupid that sounds. When I said let's get a puppy home you just be like 'no that's a bad idea' but now you are playing with puppies and getting late on the first day of university fucking wow.." Zoe said this in one take.. yes people one take.

And me and Kate were looking at her amused. And finally Kate announced we should got to the university as we don't want to be late for the first day And grab unwanted attention .

We sat in the car and drove off towards University . During the whole car ride Kate and Zoe were talking., but my mind was fully occupied with that black eyes. I tried to join their conversation but I was again drifted off to his black eyes

As we reached our university, we get off the car and look around. And it was just that typical university surrounding. Some girls in short skirts, boys in leather jackets, nerds with a book , couple smooching each other face off and etc.

We just took our bags from the car and walked towards the Administrative office to grab our time table and all. While we were walking we grabbed some attention which made me totally uncomfortable. God why can't they just move their eyes away. Idiots

As we reached Administrative office a lady was sitting there who gave us our time table and locker no. And code.Luckily our lockers were just besides each other. So we were very happy that we could spend some time together before going to classes. As we get to our lockers Zoe or I should say 'over-excited' Zoe shouted in a shrill voice

"Woah!!! Three bestie's lockers are also besties " she said.

And I just looked at my show in embarrassment and Kate was digging hole in Zoe head by her famous glare.

" Yeah and I am thinking why the hell I made you my best friend " Kate said in a sarcastic tone.

I just giggled at that and after seeing their goddamn expressions I started to laugh whole heartedly. I am telling you guys they can defeat stand up comedians with their fight. Zoe excused herself to go to the bathroom and Kate followed her shouting 'I am not finished with you yet bitch'.

I just shook my head , recovering from laughter when I saw when I was laughing people were looking at me with 'awe' expression. I just awkwardly coughed and turned towards my locker to put my books in there before I head towards the class

I was just putting my books when I felt somebody is behind me as my eyebrows frowned , someone from behind called my name Ella

I turned and was shocked to see he was that same person on whom I spilled my coffee. He was looking at me with a different expression in his eyes. Behind his there were standing to more boys , both were handsome but not as much as this Coffee guy.

"Hey! We met again" He said

"Yeah we did" I said

"So we didn't had a proper introduction, and may I do you study here too?" He asked

"Yes i study here too and My name is Ella Clark ." I said with a small smile

"Hey Ella again . I am Xavier " he said with one of his charming smirk

I just smiled and was just going to walk off when his two friends said

"How rude of me to not introduce ourself I am Aidan and this is Christian " Aidan guy said with a beautiful smile. He is cute

"You know i have a mouth and I could've introduce myself " Christian said

And just like Zoe and Kate they started to bicker too. I just giggled seeing them.

And at that time they stopped bickering at looked at me .

"Well you guys just bicker like my two best friends so." I said with giggling a little

They just turned read and Xavier just laughed at their expression . At that time bell got rang marking the classes to begin.

"It was nice meeting you all " I said with a small smile and walked from there.

I didn't have the first class with Zoe or Kate. So I was alone , I entered the class which got some attention and after some glances they went back to what they were doing .

I choosed the third seat near window. As I sat our proffesor entered the class

"Good morning students. I am Mr. Turner . Your Biology teacher. I hope you all will give your best this year and will score good marks." As he was saying door just barged opened and any guesses who entered .

Of course Xavier and his two friends. They saw me and gave me a bright smile . While made head turned towards me . I just gave them a small smile and started to concentrate in my book.

I just don't want to grab some unwanted attention .

But I do noticed how girls were looking at three with weird looks and boy with envy. I just concentrated on my books.

As they all sat very near me much to my dislike , Mr. Turner said in a angry tone.

"Mr. Knight you and your best friends are late. Classes have some rules, which you have to follow" He said

"Mr. Turner I am the one who make rules" Xavier Said in a bored tone

"Mr. Knight....umm.. class take out the page number 15 " Mr. Turner said in a scared tone

But my attention in class was long gone because the mention of Xavier's Surname.

He is The Xavier Knight. Son of the Richest person is America and I spilled my coffee over him . God save me.

I just looked at him with a frightened expression and he was looking at me with a look 'let me explain '.

I just turned my head from there because talking to such a Rich bad boy will be the last thing on earth i want to do.

God what did I put myself into.

Chapter 5

D o you guys realise when it's your birthday the next day , the clock is ticking very slow . Like you seriously want time to be run faster, 12'o clock to be stricken in clock and yayyy you celebrate your birthday. Something similar was happening with me , no guys it's not my birthday it's just that I suddenly get to know that the person whom I gave a free bath of coffee was none other than a billionaire son and can do whatever the heck he want.

I have not concentrated in class since I get to know that Xavier is a Knight. I mean oh lord , they are one of the most prestigious family in the world and me well me a simple plain girl just spilled my whole cup of coffee on him , on his shirt which I know would be way more expensive than my living expenses .

He tried to grab my attention so many times but I just ignored him. I don't know why I was ignoring him . He seemed pretty cool about it them why I was overreacting. But deep down I was scared . Scared as hell knowing he is a Knight and can make my life a living hell in a few seconds .

Class was finally over. As the class ended , I packed up my bag and was heading out of the class when my way got blocked my none other than The Xavier Knight .

I was Scared. I am definitely not denying it but I was not gonna show him that I was.

"Excuse me please I've got a class to go to" I said politely .

"Look ella , I know you are scared that I am a Knight and you practically gave me a bath of coffee would end up you in a trouble. But I promise it was fine . It was an accident. So no need to be scared " he said with a polite attitude .

"Scared me pfft.. y-you are n-not any spider I will be scared of ok?" I said trying to look brave , but I also know that I screwed up a big time with my stammering .

"OK then why you stammered twice" he said in a amusing tone with his signature Smirk.

"I-I gotta go. It was nice meeting you Mr. Knight. I am again sorry for spilling coffee on you and I hope we never get in each other's way from now on . Goodbye" I said And I was walking off when he suddenly grabbed my wrist and whispered something in my ear which made my mind gone crazy.

"But I want to cross my path with you every single day of my life, babygirl" he said in my ears.

I just looked at him in shocked and practically ran from there . I ended up in one of a stalls in girls toilet. I calmed my heart down . When finally I was composed I came out , washed my hands and started to make way towards my locker .

There were no sign of Kate and Zoe. Which means they already headed for class . I remembered it's English Lit. And we three are having it together. So I grabbed my English lit. Book and headed towards the direction of the lecture hall.

As I entered the classroom. I saw my two best friends sitting together giving me a confused look . I know why they are giving me those looks because never in my life time I would be late for a class. But today because of certain someone I got late for a class. I just shrugged and went to sit in one of the empty seats. Seat beside me was empty .

I just started to read a story in our book when a girl approached me and asked

"Would you mind , if I sit here" she asked sweetly

I just smiled and replied .

"Not at all . Please have a seat" I said

She just grinned at me and sat in the seat.

"By the way my name is Emma " she said while giving her hand for a handshake

"Nice to meet you. I am Ella" I said while shaking her hand

"Oh we both have our names starting with E " she said way too excited

I just giggled and nodded

"Can we be friends , actually it's my first day And I have no friends in here so...?" She said with sad smile

"Well who said you don't have Friends , now you have three friends " I said And called my two besties

" Hey babes, this is Emma , she is the new member of our best friends group" I stated

They grinned at each other, shook hands and welcomed her

"Did you both realized , both of your names starts with E" Zoe said

In this context, our dearest new bff , jumped in het seat and said exactly what I was thinking

"I think we have one more crackhead child to handle kate" I said to Kate for which she laughed and nodded

Emma just showed me her youngest, and throws her hands over my shoulder squeezing the shit out of Me

"OK ok enough love babe, teacher is here" I said

She detached herself from me straightened up and the class started. While the class was going on me and Emma exchanged numbers and I gave her Kate and Zoe number too.

"Okay tell me Ms. Knight who is the writer of Wuthering Heights" our teacher asked Emma suddenly

I was startled to hear that my new friend is also a Knight. But I didn't want to overreact because we both wanted to be each other's friends genuinely

I saw how she was having difficulty to answer that question so I whispered in her ears.

"Emily Brontë" she said as I whispered

"Good" Sir told and again started his lecture

When the class was over we four went out of the class together.

As we were out Emma told Me

" thank you so much Ella for helping me" she said

"Shut up girl. There's no place for sorry and thank you in our friendship " I said

She smiled and nodded

"Well girl you are a knight " Kate told her with a smirk

"Oh please Kate don't judge me on the basis of my family. I just wanna be a normal girl like you all " she said

"No one is ever gonna judge you in here girl. You are our friend and we actually don't care which family do you belong to" Zoe said And me and Kate nodded

She just hugged all three of us together and said

"Thanks you guys so much. Love you " she said

We laughed and said We love you too

And some more classes the day was finally over actually I was quite happy on how I didn't bumped into him .

After the day end we four walked towards the parking lot together.

"So girls I am going but please call me after you reach home. " Emma said while hugging us

"OK girl same applies for you and we should hang out together sometime " kare Said

We all three shouted of course and laughed

We bid our goodbye and we three and Emma went to sat in our respective cars..

When I sat in the passenger seat I saw Xavier was looking my way smiling . My eyes went wide and at that time we made our way out of the university

When I reached home , from porch I heard shouting. Which was totally new because my family was not the one who easily fights

When I went inside I saw a whole lot of scene

Mom was watching TV serial without paying any heed to my father and brother who were fighting.

They bicker back and forth , I tried to stop them but they were not stopping so I should "STOP"

they both looked at my way so finally I got the time to ask.

"Can I ask why you both made our house fish market" i said with my hands folded

"Our dearest dad in here , invited some guests" Evan said

"So what's the problem in that?" I said with raising my eye-brows

"Dad invited his bosses family who are his friends too for dinner. Who happened to be Knights . Who's son Xavier Knight happens to be my biggest Rival for God sake " and with shouting that Evan went to his room, dad towards his room and mom following dad.

I was just glued to my place from the new information I got. Knights are my dad's boss and happens to be their friends and my brother is Rival with his son , Xavier who warned me that he is not going to leave my way.

And at that moment of my life I knew I didn't screwed up big time.

I freaking Screwed up my whole life.

Chapter 6

E lla

Sometimes I feel I can handle my brother easily because he loves me so damn much that he will listen and understand what am I saying. But in the situation like this I just doubt my capability of handling my brother.

Evan have locked himself up in his room after he fought with dad over the matter of Knights coming for dinner.

I was continuously banging the door for my brother to open the door so we can talk and solve this out, but he was not listening to me. Stubborn apple(ass).

Suddenly my mom came and announced in a loud voice so that my brother can also hear,"One hour is only left for the Knights to come and Ella go get ready." she said And shooed me off towards my room.

I went towards my room , opened my wardrobe and started search for a dress. After a whole lot of searching I ended me with a white colored, mid-thigh dress . I bought it but never wore it. Finally got the chance to wear it.

I stride towards my bathroom and took a very short shower of 10 mins after I soaked water from my body and put on the dress . I did my makeup minimal as possible with a dash of mascara and nude lip stick. As I was applying perfume I heard my mom called for me informing that the guests are there.

I hurriedly combed my hair, left it down that my curls were cascading down my back and started to make my way down-stairs. I was in a hurry because I knew Evan will do lots of drama in order to come down . So atleast I should be there.

As I entered living room , I was welcomed with four faces , a man probably in his 50's . But still looks young, a women in her late 40's in a sleek black dress , Emma and Xavier. Totally expected.

As they were meeting each other, Xavier suddenly looked at my way and shock was the expression all evident on his face . Then shock melted to something else which I can't decipher. At that time my mom noticed my presence and introduced me to the Knights.

"And here is my daughter Ella " she introduced me to the guest. All looked at me and I just smiled at them . Emma was shocked to see me there and suddenly when I went to stand next to my mum , Emma hugged me and said to her mom.

"Mom this was the girl I was talking about " Emma said

"Your new friend?" Mrs. Knight asked

She nodded and grinned looking at me. I smiled at her mom and she looked at me with love and respect in her eyes.

"Well I should say Mrs. Clark your daughter is very beautiful ." she said to my mom.

I just smiled and thanked them . At that time my mom announced that dinner is ready and let's have dinner.

As we all were moving towards dining hall. I heard a whisper in my ear.

" I didn't knew you were Evan's little sister " He said with a smirk and I totally ignored him .

"Well I should say you are looking beautiful. " this time he said I looked at him with a genuine smile and of course the stupid blush.

I thanked him .

"Where is your son Samuel ?" Mr. Knight asked.

"Where's Evan Natalie?" My dad asked my mom.

She looked at me with pleading eyes so I spoke.

"He must be getting ready, I'll go and call him" I said and headed towards Evans room.

When I reached his room I saw his room was opened. So I entered his room . I saw he was smoking. He does that when he is angry. .

"Bro" I said

"Leave ella I am not coming down." he said . Well that was Rude.

"Bro please you have to come down , I know you have problems with Xavier which I am not forcing you to tell me , I just want you to know he is dad's boss and he personally called you and dad asked me to call you down , so please brother atleast for dad's reputation come down" I said.

"Ella I have a lot of things to pack , that's why I can't come down " he said and I frowned

"Where are you going? Oh wait are you leaving the house because dad's called them at our House. Please Evan don't do this please ." I said pleading . I was at the verge of crying .

"What no! I just have to go to California for some weeks I actually have some work there" he said

"Its fine I'll help you pack after the dinner. I promise" I said with a grin.

And finally my brother gave up and started to Make his way downstairs with me. I told you he will never will from me.

When we went down mom called us both to have a seat . When Xavier saw Evan he smirked at him and my brother was just about to pounce at him when I took hold of Evans forearm. God this boys and their stupidity rivalry.

We both went and sat in the dining table. We started to silently eat out dinner when suddenly Evan announced that he is going to California. Mom and dad agreed but one thing confused me was that when Evan announced he was going to California, Xavier smirked at me. I just shrugged it off and started to eat my dinner as it was Steak!! Who in the world doesn't like Steak with grilled carrot and onions.

When dinner was over we all went towards the living room. Me and Evan didn't want to but we did nevertheless.

As we reached at living room Mr. Knight spoke "Thank you for the lovely dinner Samuel and Mrs. Clark, it was delicious. "

Later rest of the three Knights thanked us too.

"Okay son have a safe flight " Mrs. Knight said to Evan and he gave her a nod and smile. Atleast he smiled. He was sitting like a robot a through the dinner.

They bid their goodbyes and was going , when my brother went towards his room I was walking them to door with my parents . I hugged Emma and said to tell her everything later and she also noticed something odd about the behavior of my brother .

When I was waving I again heard a whisper , and I freaking knew who it belonged to,

"So your brother is going out , So now i can finally have you all to myself. " Xavier said and climbed in his Lamborghini .

Now I freaking realised why he smirked at me in dining table .

Damn it!!! Or Damn me!!

Chapter 7

Ella

Every body in this world would have experienced it when at one corner of heart you are happy but in one corner you are sad. Something similar is happening with me on one side of the heart I am happy that my brother have Gone to his dream college for a national football match but in one corner of my heart I am sad that I would not be not seeing my brother for so many weeks .

Well ella it's not a thing to think right now because you brother is already in the way to California. You get your lazy ass up your bed and get ready .

I was always excited to go to study but today I was very anxious to go because of Xavier statement earlier. I really didn't want to think about him right now . I just shook my head and went towards my bathroom to get ready for the day.

I choosed a off-shoulder sky blue mid-length dress. I wore it, did a minimal make up , let my hair fall down in curls and came out of the bathroom

I started to go down when I heard a car honk . I frowned because Zoe said she will come late to university today because she had to run an errand. Kate will straight reach to school and we decided to meet their. If it was neither Zoe nor Kate then who the heck is honking in front of my house. I just wished my mom and dad good morning, took a granola bar from the fridge and went out of the house to see who was it?

And if I knew who was it and what this will lead to,I would have never came out until the car was gone.

Any guesses?Well it was Xavier, and now I was thinking why is he here? What does he want now and why is he here when he should be at University, wait is he here to pick me up? Oh my freaking ice cream. What am I gonna do now?

"Hey Love" Xavier Said while grinning from ear to ear.

"Xavier what are you doing here " I said while glancing and talking to him from his window

"To pick you up" he said in a duh tone.

"I don't want a lift Xavier, please just go from here " I pleaded him.

"I will not move an inch from here if you don't come with me" he said

"Then stand in here I am leaving bye" I said

"OK go but remember this I will stand in here and when your parents gonna come out they are going to see me , they are going to question me and I will said I came to pick you up so...." he said while smirking .

And now i was thinking he was right!! With the amount of stubbornness he had this idiotic man will stand in here and will put me in trouble .

"Okay I am going to come with you" I said

"Very good love.. the doors is always opened for you let it be cars or heart both." he said while smirking .

I just rolled my eyes on his chessy line and sat in the passenger seat.

"Well I should say you are looking beautiful " he said while looking me up and down. I blushed at that.

"Can we please leave now" I said in a bored tone.

"Your wish is my command my lady" he said and turned on the ignition .

He was driving and suddenly my stomach growled.Damn it.

"Ella did you ate your breakfast?" He said in a serious tone.

" I just had a granola bar" I said

"What? Just had a granola bar . Are u fucking kidding me , you should have a proper breakfast . You should take care of yourself love" he said with concern dripping from his voice .

"I am sorry" I didn't knew why I was apologizing to him but his concern towards me really overwhelmed me. Apart from my best friends and family no one ever showed a concern towards me.

"We will have breakfast first then we will go to university and no discussions over it." he said with finality in his voice

I smiled and nodded.

We reached a cafe to eat our breakfast.. I giggled seeing that Cafe. It was looking luxurious but yet homey and comfy at the same time.

"Why are you laughing love?" He said in amused tone.

"Well you being you I thought I particularly need to beg you to not take me to any seven star restaurant." I said while smiling at him.

He just rolled his eyes amusedly and we came out of his car

As we were walking towards Cafe some boys looked at me in a weird way . Xavier glared at him in a very dangerous way and wrapped his arm on my waist possessively .

We entered the Cafe and we sat on a table near window. Xavier was still angry but he didn't want to show me so he clenched his hand in a fist and was looking out of the window. I don't know why I just had a instinct that I should calm him down. So I just placed my hand on his fist he looked at my hand while was small in comparison to his fist and suddenly he took hold of my hand in a tight grip but not that tight to hurt me. His hold was just claiming like I was his. This Alpha man really needs a chill pill.

I just wanted to calm his mood and lighten the moment .

"So are we going to eat something or not?" I said

He just looked at me and smiled and called the waiter .

The waiter came and started to look at me up and down . I shifted in my seat weirdly.

"you are fired " Xavier Said in a super angry tone

He started to stutter but he gave one look from which he ran away.

This time a lady came and took our order professionally

"You know you can't just fire anybody" I said

"Well I can when I am the owner son or you should say next boss." he said smirking.

"Yeah right" I said nodding realising that Knights own almost everything in New York and around the world.

After having our breakfast we went towards his car and started to drive towards University .

On the way to University, I just thought how he was so concerned, considerate , calm , composed and loving with me. Should I gave this thing which is between us a chance .

As we reached University , he and I both came out of his car and I turned back towards him to thank him when I saw he was standing there looking confused .

"Do you wanna say something " I asked

"Yes" he said

"Go on"

He released a sigh and Said

"Ella will you please go on a date with me?" he asked me .

And i was shocked. This handsome man in here was asking me for a date. But how can I say no to him when he had been so good with me..

"Yes" I said

He grinned wide and hugged me and said.

"Tomorrow is weekend I'll pick you up today at 8 from your home . Bye" he said and jogged towards University .

I just stood there smiling and shaking my head and suddenly my all smiled disappeared when I realised .

I was going on a date with my brother's Rival.

Oh Shit. I am doomed. In a good way though.

Chapter 8

E lla

They say when life gives you lemons, you make a kool-aid. And something similar I was feeling today . During the whole day there was zero percent of my concentration in any of the classes , whole time I was thinking about mine and xavier's date. I still cant believe I, Ella Clark is going on a date with the most popular guy of this school, who is soon going to be the CEO of the most successful company in USA and last but the bomb , He is my brothers Rival. I should pat my back for making this decision.

But how hard I Try to have some feelings for Xavier, I have it. Nobody can do anything what you feel towards a person Right?. I feel Safe, secure, beautiful and protected with him. He makes me feel loved. Well that's a foreign feeling for me so I don't know what is love? But it's just that what I read it in books when you feel yourself with that person it's love. And that's what exactly i was feeling for Xavier.

I really wanted to go on a date with Xavier and now I am finally going but in deep down in my heart I am afraid of the consequences our where-to-headed relationship will bring and mostly how my brother will react.

I have always done what my brother choosed for me. I trusted him blindly and his commands were my final words. But once in my 19 years of existence I wanted to follow what my heart says and Yes I am going to follow what my heart say without thinking about any consequences that It will bring.

I got up from my bed as i returned 2 hours ago. It's 5:40 pm now which mean maximum 2 hours to get ready. I got up from the bed to select a dress and get ready . After a whole lot of half an hour I selected a Biege colour short dress. It was beautiful and I kept it to Wear in a special occasion, well I think the special occasion came.

I wore it , combed my hair into beautiful loose curls and did a nude make-up. By the time I was ready it was 07:50. Ok now I was getting nervous. Oh my God, where would he be taking me, what we will do Oh god.

At strike of clock at 8, my doorbell rang . Thankfully my mom and dad have gone to a party and would not return until tommorow so i was home alone.

I made my way towards the door and here he was standing in all his glory in a black suit. Looking at me with a weird emotion in his eyes. He checked me from up and down and I took this chance to check him too. Jesus, He is hot!!!

"You look beautiful love" he said with a beautiful smile

"You don't look so bad of yourself" I said with a shy expression

He just laughed at my expression and tilted my chin up

"I brought something for you" he said And walked towards his car.

I just stood in my position, what did he brought for me. I hope it's not something So expensive I couldn't accept. I hope it's just a flower or something.

He returned and stood behind my back suddenly he took all my hair from my back and put it on my left shoulder,I felt his hot breath fanning on my neck . In spur of a moment he clasped a beautiful pendant in my neck. When I look at it ,from the first view I understood it would be expensive.

" I am sorry Xavier but I can't accept this. This Is way too much expensive for my liking and I really don't deserve this" I said

"You deserves the world Ella and if you return this pendant to me my heart will be broken" he said pouting .

I just laughed at his cuteness and look at him still doubted.

"Please accept this" he said while holding my hand and looking at me with puppy dog eyes. How can I resist him.

"Okay!! No more expensive gifts ever" I said

"I can't promise love ." he said in a teasing tone

I just rolled my eyes and he fake glared at me.

"Shall we leave?" He asked with his right hand out for me

I looked at his hand then at him. I smiled and replied

"We shall" I said placing my left hand into his large ones.We walked hand in hand towards his car and him like being a gentleman opened the car door for me , I told him a small thank you and sat in the passenger seat of his expensive sports car.

He turned and came to sit on the driver's seat and turned on the ignition.

"Where are we going?" I asked him

"That's for me to know and you to find out" he said

"Oh come on , i am just curious " I said

"Curiosity killed the Cat, love" he said teasingly

I just pouted and slumped back in my seat.

"Can you please stop pouting?" He said to me out of the air

"Why?" I said with eyebrows frowned.

"Because I wouldn't be able to control myself from kissing you senselessly if you keep doing that" he stated.

I just blushed and looked away from him. During the whole car ride we were silent, but it was not awkward it was a comfortable one.

After I think one hour we reached Nowhere!!!

"What is this place Xavier, it looks like forest" i asked him

" do you trust me" he asked

"Of course I do" I said

"If you do, then just take a hold of my hand and let me lead where I am leading you" he said

I just nodded . He opened my door, gave me his hand I placed my hand in his and he pulled me out. He took hold of my hand tightly and started leading me to God knows where

After walking for I think 20 minutes. Trees were suddenly decreasing and we reached a spot while literally took my breaths away .

Here it was in the middle of the forest and beautiful decorated table with lots of food in it

"Shall we eat " he asked

"Oh yeah. I am famished" I said to him.

He lead me to the table, pulled out the chair for me and we started to eat.

"Did you like it?" he asked

"Its Italian and its My favorite " I replied .

"Same here" he said

We finished our dinner and I thought we were leaving when he took hold of my hand and took me somewhere.

It was a live theater in the forest playing Me Before You. My favorite movie.

"Let's watch a movie " he said

I excitedly nodded.

We were at the end of the movie and soon movie got finished. When movie finished I turned to look at Xavier when I saw he was already looking at me . Suddenly he started to lean in and I started to lean in too. I liked my lips and now his eyes were on my lips now. Suddenly he put his lips on my . After good amout of 10 seconds I realized he is kissing me. Oh god I didn't kissed him back immediately but when I gained my consciousness I started to kiss him back.

God that kiss is something, it is doing so many things to me . My body is on fire. He grabbed my waist to pull me closer and now I was half of his lap. His kiss was like a drug , one can't get enough of it but I had to go because I was out of breath.

We pulled apart and we both rested our foreheads against each other and suddenly he said so unexpected that I didn't know it will turn my life upside down .

"I like you" he said catching his breath

I looked at him in the eyes I was about to say something one he shut me up .

"Let me complete my sentence. You are the first girl who ever caught my attention. Before you I didn't care about any girls feeling, I would date them for fun and dump their heart without thinking about them for once . But since the moment I saw you I saw my whole life in front of my eyes. I thought love at first sight thing is a total absurd thing but when I saw you I get to know why people love someone so much. I love you ella , I really do . Never think that I am playing with you because If anytime I would hurt you I'll die because I love you that much. You are the only person I dream when I sleep , only person who wakes me up because I want to see you and only person I want to spend each day of mine. " he completed his speech. It was definitely not a sentence.

By the end of his confession tears were streaming down my face . He wiped away all my tears and said,

"My girl's tears are expensive, don't waste them on a stupid lovesick man ranting." he said while laughing .

"You know it was the most sweetest thing I ever heard. Or anyone ever said to me" I said.

"Be mine" he said while smiling. I looked at him shocked.

"Be mine . Give me the privilege to call you mine" he said with a pleading look.

I looked into his eyes and I just can't say no to him . I don't know what consequences of my this decision will bring into our Life. But this man sitting in front of me is everything I ever wanted or ever wished for. He was a blessing .

"I'll be yours. " I said while shaking my head for a yes.

He suddenly crashed his lips on mine and we again kissed for some

We were sitting in each other's embrace for quite a long time when I said I want to go back home.

During the whole car ride we had big grin over our face and he kept holding my hand.

When we reached our house i turned around towards him.

"Thank you for everything" I said

"Anything for my girl " he said

I smiled and I was about to go when he pulled me and crashed his lips on mine. It was a passionate kiss .

When we pulled apart I gave him a questioning look.

He answered "helps me sleep at night." Still smiling goofily..

I just laughed at him and get off the car. I looked at him and waved towards him and entered the house. I straight went to my room to change in my night dress.

When I changed my dress and came back. I thought Xavier must have reached his home. Suddenly my phone pinged with messages.

"Good night girlfriend . Dream of me ;)"

I blushed reading it and replied

"Good night boyfriend. No I would still still stick to Cedric Diggory :)" I already knew he would be having a pout on his face with that line. God that man-child.

With switching my phone off. I laid down in my bed. Today was hectic as well as one of the most precious day of my life.

While laying down I thought. For the first time in lifetime I listened to my Heart and not my brother. I kind of feel guilty for not doing what my brother told me to do. To stay away from Xavier but I couldn't . I can't hurt him and most importantly I can't hurt myself but detaching myself from him.

But this time that feeling got vanished, because for the first time in forever I am doing what I want to do and that is being with Xavier.

Chapter 9

Ella

Things in my life was always been planned out at what age what I want to do. But due to the sudden entry of someone my world did a 180^0 revolution and a very unexpected thing happened with me . Girl which didn't had a boyfriend since forever now have a boyfriend. Just wow.

Everyday I just wake up simply but today I waked up with a smile on my face . I danced-walked my way till my wardrobe and started to pick out a dress . I don't know everyday I just pick out any dress but today I want to look special well should I add for special someone .

I choosed a burgundy colored Skirt with a black strip top and accompanied it with black shoes..

I got ready and today I was in a very happy mood so I made my way towards dining table with a smile on my face.

Good morning mum" I wished my mom while kissing in the cheek

"Good morning " she said with a confused smile

"Good morning dad" I said while back hugging my dad

"Good morning, you seem very happy princess" Dad said

"Because i am" I replied while sitting on the dining table to eat my breakfast

"Well that's good" dad said and mom and I nodded .

When I was eating my breakfast I heard horns.

"I think Zoe is here to pick me up. I am full. Bye dad Bye mum" I said while running towards door

As I came out I thought I will come face to face with zoe's car but here he was, my handsome Boyfriend. Leaning in his car door looking at me

I just shared my head with a smile and approached him

"Good morning love" he wished me with a forehead kiss

"Good morning " I replied while blushing

"Your chauffeur at you service madamè " he said with a fake French accent.

I just giggled and sit inside the car. He in just a spare of a second came and said down in driving seat and we made our way towards University .

"I thought Zoe was going to pick me up" I said while playing with his finger as he placed his hands upon my thigh while driving .

"I told her that we are dating and from now I will pick you up." he simply said

" YOU WHAT!!!!" I shouted

"Damn love I want us both alive" he said while getting the car back on track as it got off-track .

" You said Zoe that we are dating and by this time I think Kate knows too and I didn't told them directly . God I am doomed" I said

" it's ok love I will save you" he said while pecking my lips .

I just blushed and sat in my seat . When we reached at University, we came out together which gathered a lot of attraction. I thought I would let him go first but he suddenly pulled and entwined our fingers together and we made our way to our lockers all the while I was blushing .

When we both approached locker i was welcome with two beautifully annoyed faces of Zoe ,Kate and Emma.

They approached us and started shouting at us for not telling them . God they are being so noisy. Till now I think everybody knows I am dating Xavier. While Kate and Zoe are giving me a lecture of friendship rules, Emma is ripping his brother brain of that it was his duty to tell her as she is his sister .

"Guys we have just started to date yesterday you all are just making a fuss out of it . So, If you three and all those people standing in here who are waiting for our official statement on our relationship. So, yes I am dating this beautiful girl beside me named Ella Clark. Those who want to create a fuss, can disturb me no problem with but if anyone ask or say anything heck even breathe near my girl I'll literally break every fucking bone of your body and you all know once I say something I literally mean it." Xavier said coldly with a dead stare directed towards everybody who were standing in crowd .

"The show is over people" Chris said as he approached us. He and Aidan first gave a hug to Xavier and then me. Crowd also scurried away .

"Hey there sister-in-law" they both said in unison while smirking.

Kate, Zoe and Xavier just laughed while I just blushed and slapped their arms .

After our little moment at our lockers we all headed to our classes. Me and Chris had a class together and rest all were together in AP. Me and Chris approached class together and he selected seat for both of us. We were talking when teacher came and class started .

After our classes we all met at the canteen . As I approached canteen as I was the last because my last class was not with anybody of our group. I saw all my friends sitting in a table together being the centre of attraction of everybody.God Help me!

When they saw me they shouted that they already bought my food and I have no need to stand in a line. When I got to them they were having a serious discussion over something So I asked while sitting next to Xavier who pecked me in cheek.

"So can I ask what discussion is going over here" I asked while eating fries from my boyfriends plate which he doesn't seem to mind at all nevertheless he is feeding me more.

"We are discussing over the football match tommorow, you are coming right ella ? Our Xavier needs support ." Aidan said while smirking while acting all innocent battling his eyelashes.

"What football match?" I asked while looking towards Xavier

.

"There is our football match tommorow and I would really like if you would come to my match tommorow wearing My jersey. " he said

I was unsure about it so I was just fidgeting with my words .

"Please" he said pouting.

"Okay" I can't bear over his cuteness and told him that i will come. Everybody in here banged table.

After our classes got over, we all met at parking lot.

"Sorry baby I can't drop you off at your home,I have to practice for the match tommorow or else my coach will sue me" Xavier apologized.

I just told him no need of any sorry and kissed his cheek . I said bye to everyone and promised I will come tommorow and will meet them before match . I sat in Zoe's car and headed towards home.

Tommorow me and Xavier are going to make our relationship official. We will be officially a couple in front of everybody. I am going to wear his jersey and for the first time I am going to see a football match and that too of my boyfriend who also happened to be the team captain.

God help me tommorow or I'll be doomed! Oh god how can I be excited and scared at same time . Well let's just say Pros and Consof being most popular boy of University's Girlfriend. Hectic I know.

Chapter 10

Ella

The day of the football matched arrived. I am literally telling you guys my hands are sweating, there are so many reasons behind it. It's the first time I am going to see a football match, it's the first time in forever that I have a boyfriend that too the university football team captain and me having an anxiety attack right now think about all this things seems normal thing.

Me the most un-morning person in whole universe got up extra early today, did my morning routine and from that time I am standing in front of my closet to choose a outfit for me. You must be thinking that Zoe and kate are there to help me but no these two girls, when I need them the most have wore an invisible cloak. I just got a message from Zoe saying 'Xavier will not be able to pick you up today, so as your bestie I will give you a lift' . I just laughed at this text and replied OK.

This outfit choosing things on what to wear today are the most difficult things . When I was 16 I knew I am not going to be a fashion icon. Well all the dresses that I have in my closet are either bought by my friends, mom or Olivia.

So I looked into the closet to find a perfect wear for today. I have to wear his jersey which he will give me before game so I choose a simple outfit so that I can easily wear his jersey .

I chose a black jeans with a pink sweatshirt combining with my adidas shoes. I called Zoe to pick me up as I was ready. I went downstairs and my mom and dad were not at home as they both are visiting my uncle and aunt in Miami. I went down took a granola bar and at that just in time Zoe honked her horn.

I went outside and sat in her car. I wished good morning to both of them. We shoot towards University. In the way we talked about how the team which were competing with Our team. That team is really a strong one.

We reached University just in time. All faces were very excited for the game today . I was specially finding a face but I couldn't be able to find it.

When we three entered University, everyone were giving me weird looks, some with fear , some with anger and some with jealousy. Emma ran towards me and hugged me and said We all should follow her as she saved a seat at bleachers for us. We were following her but suddenly by my elbow I was pulled into a room , I was going to shout when the persons hand covered my mouth.

When in fear I looked at the person it was my handsome Boyfriend smiling at me .

"Hey" he said as he removed his hand from my mouth

"You just scared me to death. What are you doing?" I said smiling and pulling his ears lightly.

"You are looking so beautiful " he said while tucking a strand of hair behind my ear.

"Thank you. And where is my jersey" I said with a sassy attitude extending my hand towards him.

"Oh already stating rights on my things love, atleast could've waited till our marriage." he said in a teasing manner.

I blushed hard.

"Are u gonna give it or not." I said raising my eyebrows at him.

"Here it is." he said while taking out it from a paperback he was holding .

I took it from his hand and wore it instantly. I tucked it so it wouldn't look baggy. When I looked at Xavier after waiting I saw a different emotions dancing in his eyes. And first time I could decipher it, it was love,adoration.

"I love you." he whispered

"I like you too a lot more than I could ever tell you. " I said

I know it sounds odd when he states he loves me and me being replying by I like him but let's just say I can't lie about my feelings and right now I am not sure whether I love this amazing man . I am 99% sure about it but oh that 1% sucks.

With my confession he landed his lips on mine , he kissed me for few minutes after which he pulled away . I just raised my eyebrow at him in which he shrugged and said.

"For winning the match love. Protein shake. You wouldn't know? ." he said teasingly.

I just laughed and said that he should go if not he will be late for the game today . He just pecked my lips and ran towards the field . I straightened myself and started to make my way towards bleachers and my friends. When I was in the field and when everyone saw me in captains jersey I literally heard so many gasps all where throwing daggers at me . Some people looked amused and some angry .

I made my way towards my friends who were smirking I just shook my head and sat in my seat. As I sat both the team entered to start the match.

When Xavier entered my friends intentionally coughed and that made me blushed.

After Xavier and all teams member shook hands with the opposite team . Xavier started to turn his head here and there as he was finding someone . And his eyes landed on me , he just winked at me and literally I heard some aww's from the crowd.

Aidan and chris saw us too and they waved their hands at us.

The match started our team was doing great and at the half time of the game I knew we were going to win . And as I said our team won.

After our team win they hugged each other and suddenly Xavier started to make his way towards the crowd. I got as to why he was doing that. And suddenly he came and hugged me. I just smiled and hugged him back. Though he was sweaty but he still smelled like my Xavier.

He just whispered in my ears"I always knew you were my lucky charms. I love you"

I just smiled and hugged him tighter.

After the game got finished and every one shared congratulations. Boys freshened up and now we were making our way towards our car.

"So guys you all coming for celebration party right?" Chris said

"No No you all go I am just heading home. You all go and enjoy bye. " i said

Xavier looked at me and smiled and said

"You guys go I am going to spend some quality time with my beautiful girlfriend. " he said as he wrapped his hand on my waist.

Everyone looked at us and smirked.

"Please use protection if you decides to do that. We all are too young for being uncles and aunts." Chris said smirking.

Xavier just smirked at me and smacked chris head. He started to lead me towards the way to his car. He opened the door for me we all sat and started to make way to God knows where

.

"So where are we going?" I asked him while he was driving while holding my hands in his palm.

"Some place where I will show how much i love you." he whispered in my ears and bit it lightly. And God he was driving

I just blushed and looked straight at the road, leaning in my seat.

This boyfriend of me really makes me fall for him day by day.

Chapter 11

E lla

As you all know that I have a very handsome Boyfriend who doesn't like to listen to me that's why he is not telling me where are we going for past half an hour.

"Xavier for the last time I am asking where are we going" I asked him for the nth time.

"And I am telling you for the nth time I am not going to tell you." He said with his stupid signature smirk.

I just slumped back in my seat and pouted.

"Don't pout Ella ,or I will not be able to control myself " he said And with that statement my stupid blood rushed up to my face and I was flushed .

He just chuckled at my reaction and again started to concentrate on driving.

Suddenly car stopped, as I was a long drive I dropped my eyes closed so when car suddenly stopped I opened my eyes and saw the most beautiful cottage house ever.

That cottage house was so beautiful that even Cinderella and Snow white will be jealous of the cottage in front of them . It looked like it straight came from a fairy tale.

It wasa semi-sized cottage neither too big nor too small , just of perfect size. It was decorated with fairy lights, lantern and had a very beautiful garden around it.

I was so mesmerized with the beauty of that cottage I didn't noticed Xavier came around and was giving me his hand for me to come out of the car.

I took his hand and came out of the car.

"Did you like it?" He asked me

"Like it I loved it" I said

"I bought it for you." he confessed

"You didn't have to." I said while getting overwhelmed .

"I had to." he said

"Why?" I asked. Tears were already gathered up in my eyes. And I swear his sweetness was just about to make me cry.

"I love you" he confessed and that bring tears spill out of my eyes.

This was the guy I was waiting for whole in my life, the one I was waiting for , my prince charming, my knight in shining armour, and at that exact moment I realised how much I loved him. I was so blinded by my stupid assumptions about not being sure but I was in love with him since forever. And I need to tell him . He needs to know it.

I was about to confess it when he dragged me to the cottage, it was beautiful from inside too. It was huge but comfy at the same time. I loved it.

The arrangements he did inside the cottage will be somethingthat I would never forget in my entire life. He set up a table how I like. It was so beautiful that it will literally make someone cry.

He gave me his hand to lead me towards the table.

"My girl favourite Italian food." he said while he pulled out the chair for me.

Everything was according to my taste. If this guy doesn't love me then nobody does. He was perfect in everything.

We talked and ate our dinner. Suddenly he became very serious . Like he was to confess to me about something. Something he wanted to talk about from long time as he was looking unsure.

"Ella, I know you don't love me but it's just that if you are thinking that I am playing with you so just please think that I am not playing with you. How much I love you i don't think i ever loved anybody that much?. I literally can't live without you. I know you don't love me but i will make sure you fall in love with me because i am so much in with you . I love you so much." his confession was so pure and so good but his one line made me realize my 1% shit. And my shit loose.

"Who the hell told you I don't love you huh? You are the only person I love blindly, only person who care for me apart from my family without wanting anything in return . How much you made me feel special in past few days I don't think anybody really did. And if you think think that I don't love you well then keep in your mind that Xavier I love you to moon and back and even world can't stop me from loving you. You are my one true love. I know you are very much annoying but I am the only one who can bear your stubbornass. And if you say once more that I don't love you I'll kiss your ass goodbye." I confessed partially shouting at him.

"Y-you love m-me?" he stuttered for the first time.

And that's when I realised I just told him that I love him.

I just blushed and nodded.

He lifted Me up my seat and swirled me around .

"I can't believe the person I love the most also love me back" he said twirling me around .

He slowly put me down while I just giggled at him .

After that suddenly he pressed his lips on mine and I realised he was kissing me. This kiss held so many emotions it was not only physical but emotional . That kiss held so many emotions. He was passionately kissing me and I was kissing the man I love the most back.

This Day can't get any better. I love this man so much.

Chapter 12

E lla

It's not everyday that The Ella Clark woke up with a smile on the face but today was that day i woke up with a beautiful smile on the face anyone can guess why well the guess is simple only because of my dearest handsome Boyfriend. And his yesterday's suprise.

After our beautiful date yesterday Xavier dropped me home , he asked me to have a good night sleep , gave me a forehead kiss and drove off. But I was never able to sleep. How the heck will it reach when you have such a handsome Boyfriend who you don't know what shock will give you.

I had classes next day so i slept for few hours and now here I am getting ready for the day. I chose my outfit already.

I chose a mom jeans with white strap top and wore a grey cardigan over it. I took my bag, phone and went towards the dining table. I wished mom and dad good morning , i ate my breakfast and as I just finished at that time I heard a honk of a car . I wore my sneakers and ran off to see my Xavier was honking his car with a beautiful grin up his handsome face .

I ran and sat in the passenger seat as i sat he pecked me in my lips and wished me good morning I reciprocated his wish and we took off towards the car.

We were having a comfortable conversation when xavier said something .

"So our school is having a spring dance ball dance event day after tomorrow so today and tommorow every one would be busy for its preparation . Everybody is only allowed with a date with them as it is a ball date." he said awkwardly.

Oh god don't tell me he is asking me...

"So?" I said But my inside were dancing and rolling like in any second my heart will explode.

"So would you like to be my date for the event?" he asked hopefully.

"Are you sure?" I asked

He just laughed at my sentence.

"Yeah I am super unsure to take my lovely girlfriend to the ball." He said raising his one eyebrow at me.

"Thank you for the sarcasm baby." I said .

At that sudden time I jumped up in my seat and started to shout and squeal. He just looked at me and laughed like I am an idiot . Well i am so happy that I was not able to control myself.

Xavier

The girl dancing and jumping in my passenger seat really let me doubt that how the hell can I be so fucking lucky. Like she is the only happiness and sunshine in my life. God really gave me the best gift of my entire life. She is the most beautiful girl I've ever met and I am so happy to call her Mine.

Everyday with her I feel so lucky, happy and everyday I really feel I am falling in love with her more and more. I am so in love with her more than yesterday. Sometime I just look at her picture in my wallpaper and smile to myself, Chris and Aidan call me Whipped ass about it, but I don't give two shits about it because deep down i also know that I am whipped over her . I am so in love with her .

Before I met her I was never a person who believed in Love but after meeting her I realised what is the meaning of love, what is that feeling when you feel that this person standing in from of you is the person you want to spend your rest of your life with. For me Ella is that person.

"Yes yes yes" she suddenly shouted . Oh god she agreed to go to ball with me . Well i pray this would be her answer when I will propose her. Let's hope for the best dude. No negative thoughts are needed between me and my El.

We reached University, and got off the car together we got some stares from which Ella was quite oblivious as she was holding my arm tightly and telling me about the new book she is reading .I just glare at them which let them turn their gaze away from me and my girl.

Me and ella went towards the locker and saw our all friends together. Well i think that Aidan has something for Zoe I don't know but whenever I see him seeing her I see a spark in his eyes . I don't know but i think they'll make a good couple .

When we reached them Ella greeted them all and all of them greeted us too. Zoe and Kate were blushing so I didn't knew why they literally dragged Ella with them . Thank god I got the chance to peck Ella in the forehead . My day would've been bad if I didn't.

After that they went towards Classes as the bell rang. At that sudden time stident council leader of our university which was some Nerd announced all the boys to gather in the auditorium for the celebration prepations.

Well everybody is going to get a heart attack as Xavier Knight is not a guy to bring a date with him but this time he have one now. I was a fling guy. Come on you all know me.

"Hey ! Do you both have date to the ball tommorow?" I asked Aidan and Chris

They just looked at each other, smirked shrugged and went towards the auditorium .

"You know nothing Xavier Knight." They both said and walked away.

Chapter 13

T hird person POV

Ella, Zoe and kate were in top of the moon. You all know why Well you already know that Xavier asked Ella out from the ball, but the fun part is Zoe and kate also have date this time. Any guesses? . Stupid of me , it's a very easy guess they both have been asked my Chris and Aidan . Zoe have been asked by Aidan and kate by chris and fortunately they both agreed to go on a date with them.

So this is what they brought them here from 3 hours getting ready for the ball party . The theme Noir El Blanc . So these three chose black dresses. Straight after university yesterday they went to the mall together to get their ball gowns.

Now they were getting ready in their respective ball gowns.

"Ella Do you have a hair pin?" kate asked as she was tying her hair

Ella passed it from her drawer.

"Kate can you please zip up my dress " Zoe asked Kate.

And that way they all were helping each other to get ready for the ball.

In morning as it was holiday at University because of the ball and all the boys were busy with the preparations but they didn't forgot to message all three that they will be picking them up at 7:00 pm and all three couples will go together .

Finally after getting ready for 3 hours it was 6:45 so only 15 minutes before boys will be there. Girls turn around to look at each other. Well they all were looking like goddess.

Ella's Dress

Zoe's dress

Kate's dress

Ella:

At the strike of 7 our doorbell rang . My mom went and opened the door and I heard mom interacting with them. We just look at each other , grabbed our purse and we went downstairs.

We were not able to go downstairs together and faster because of the heavy ball gown and the heels. So one by on We all reached downstairs.

When we reached downstairs We were shocked to see my mom and dad were interacting with the boys friendly.

I thought my mom and dad would freak out by seeing Xavier Knight at our doorstep. But they were very friendly with him like he is not my brothers Rival.

They were friendly talking not giving a damn about the outer world so Zoe just coughed so we could grab their attention. And damn my man was looking outstanding .when the boys saw us they froze. I thought we were looking good, but from their expressions it was confirmed we were looking awesome .

Suddenly they walked toward us Zoe and Aidan shared a hugged and Chris and Kate shared a hand gesture . My Man suddenly came and pecked Me in my lips. God my parents were just standing beside us and he freaking kissed me. I think world is going to miss Xavier Knight.

But when I looked towards my parents instead of a angry expression full of rage they seem happy. God are they happy about my relationship with Xavier or heck they are also breaking rules like me to not date my brothers rival . I think the later one was correct.

"What young lady you thought that we will not get to know if you will not tell us who you are dating huh? " My mom asked with keeping a smug face.

"Uh uh mom I umm i " I stuttered

"Oh leave it ! We knew there is something going between you two from the first day ge came to pick you up" Dad said. My mouth fell open and I was speechless. How the hell did they know that. I don't know.

All were looking at me with a smirk so I just closed my eyes breathed in and said .

"I think we are getting late" I said as I dragged Xavier out of my house.

I heard mom and dad laughs .

After we came out we all looked at each other and started to laugh. God that was heck funny and embarrassing .

After out little laughter session. We all were walking towards were boys were talking us. After few steps we reached and what i saw freaking made my eyes go wide as saucer.

"A freaking Limousine " Zoe and kate shouted in unison. .

"Yes a Limo . It's Xavier's . Thought we all would go in a single car to the event " Aidan said.

We just shook our heads and I turned to Xavier who was looking at me with a smirk and he winked at me. Filthy rich I am telling you guys.

After that we were lead towards the limo and we all went off towards the event.

When we reached the event Xaviers driver parked the car and we all came out . Boys help us to do so.

All eyes were on us when we entered. Like literally I was feeling like I was a famous celebrity. It was very overwhelming.

When we entered the event , it was a typical how a ball should be type of event.

We entered and at that sudden time principal mam walked up to podium and started the event.

When we reached Emma approached us with Rick her date. He was a cool and good boy. We all were drinking champagne when Xavier whispered in my ears.

"I want you to meet someone " he whispered after looking into my eyes.

"Guys excuse us " I said

And we walked off towards where Xavier was leading me

We reached a spot where a couple were standing , they looked so elegant and sophisticated.

"Mom Dad, Ella is here to meet you." Xavier Said

Oh freaking lord he brought me to meet his parents . In front of whole freaking university.

The couple turned around and looked at us with a smile . Suddenly the lady hugged me and after her the man to hugged me. I was freezed but I hugged them back.

"Oh I've been waiting so long to meet you. We only met on that dinner at your house But this idiot of my son was not bringing you home. By the way I didn't got time to introduce myself personally to you on that day sweetie. Pardon for that. I am Patricia knight and he is my husband Nathan Knight. " he introduced.

"Pleasure to meet you both Mr. And Mrs. Knight .

"Oh no need of any formality sweetie , we are practically a family." his mother said.

After that we sat in their table , our friends also came and we all started to talk happily . I sometime felt Xavier looking at me with loving eyes which easily made me blush .

After three hours or something Event was going to get over and I wanted air as it was now really suffocating me. In that long dress and all.

I went outside and Xavier followed me.

"Do you like them?" Xavier asked referring to his parents.

"They are the most beautiful and kind couple I met in my whole life." I said

He looked at me with a so in love expression and placed his lips on mine suddenly

After our kiss he placed his forehead against mine and said.

"This day can't get any better" I just smiled and he placed a loving peck on my forehead.

But deep in my mind I have that thought that peace is going to end soon. Something is going to happen . I was scared but i didn't want to show it as everything was so perfect. So I just shook my head and let that thought fade away. But the harder I try there is one thought keep invading in my mind

'This is the silence before the strom'.

Chapter 14

E van

It's been so many days I have been out of my home. I really miss my family especially my baby sis. I am used to her presence but not feeling her around me for almost 3 months is really pissing me off. Today is the last day of my seminar and after that I'll be flying off towards my home and meet my family. When I came from home I was really pissed of because of him that fucking Xavier Knight.

I really don't understand why did he have to be our family friend out of all people in the world . I was ready having a hard time in my house with him and I fucking looked the way he was looking at my sister. But i just don't really understand why ella was blushing while looking or I should glancing at him . Maybe I was just hallucinating. My ella will not in near of someone whom I hate.

So after freaking three months , I am going back home . I am so excited to go back my home. I brought many gifts for my family especially ella.

She never asked Any gift from me but i really like giving her gifts. I bought some dresses , shoes, jewellery for her. I love her so much . I know she is the only person in the entire who will never ever betray me. I trust and love her so much. I can do anything for her.

As I was packing my suitcase I got a call from Tyler he is one of my friend and team mate from basketball team .I got confused as to why he is calling me I picked up the call to hear what he have to say

"Hey man" I said

"Do you really know what going on behind your back man?" he said

"Whats going on " I asked confused as to what is going on

"Man you really don't know what is going on? " He asked

"No I dont" I said With a very impatient voice

"God! Your dearest sister whom you trust the most in the entire world is dating your biggest Rival Xavier Knight behind your back . They both are dating, chilling , kissing and hanging out man." he said

"What the fuck are you talking about Tyler white. My sister can't do that to me. " I shouted at him

"If you don't trust me you will trust the pictures I have of them right " he said And cut the call.

He send me soms pictures when I downloaded and opened it I saw my sister kissing , and having fun with my dearest Rival.

My whole world crashed down at me . I was just not believing that something like this my sister could do to me whom I trusted the most in this world.

I just sat down on my bed and my phone slid off my hand and hot the floor and broke into million of pieces.

I was shocked to my core as to why she did this. Didn't I told her to not go anywhere near him and heck she is dating him .

And that Xavier how the hell he got so many guts to date my sister. I will kill him . I will definitely do.

And I will also not sphere Ella for this mistake for sure.

I landed onto the airport and marched towards the car in total anger I was in so much rage that I was seeing all red.

I just went towards my cab and told the driver to take me to ella's university. I am not going to leave that Xavier.

As I reached their university I marched towards the gate , when I reached there i asked on the students where is that fucking Xavier and he said that he is in football ground practicing .

I just marched towards football ground I am not going to leave him .

As I reached football ground I saw him practising , all members of football team saw me so the cleared the way for Me to go . He was still oblivious of my presence. When I reached near him he turn around. At first his jaw clench and then he got confused as to why i am approaching him . Well take that asshole .

I just landed a punch at his face and was continuously land-ing punches on his face.

"Why the fuck you are punching me" he said while defending himself from my punches.

I just landed another punch and said

"That's for dating my sister you motherfucker" I shouted

I am not going to let him live another day.

Chapter 15

E^{lla}

My life was going like a cakewalk. A handsome man as my boyfriend who love and care for meand protect me from everything. I just love him . How can somebody can't he is so perfect.

Everything is going very perfectly but somewhere in tge back of my mind I have a feeling that something is going to happen. I don't really know what it is but I surely know that something is going to happen.

Currently I was in cafeteria with Zoe and Kate waiting for the boys . We were chit chatting about some topic when the door of the cafeteria was barged opened by none other than Chris and what he said really made my knees go weak.

"Ella your brother is beating the shit out of Xavier " he said to me while panting.

I just ran towards the ground without giving a second glance at the people who were calling my names. Oh my God why Evan is beating Xav, did something happened between those two. But, if something happened Xavier would've told me but he never mentioned anything about Evan to me.

When I reached the football ground I saw my brother and boyfriend having a heartclench match. I was so in shock that I freezed in my place. I was unable to move. My friends joined me . They also gasped while seeing the match. We all didn't know what to do.

At that exact time Aidan ran towards us said to me.

"Ella your brother is beating the shit of Xavier because he got to know that he is dating you" he said.

And at that exact moment my world stop. Evan my brother is beating a man to pulp just because I love him and I am dating him . I love my brother the most, but he have no rights to control my life. Heck how can he beat someone whom I love.

I was so in rage that I started to walk towards Evan and Xavier. I am so pissed off with Evan that the world can't stop me from shouting at him.

I love Evan . He is one of the most important person I my life and this is what he did to me. Evan why did you do this. I didn't realised but some drops of tears came out of my eyes.

When I reached there I heard my brother shouting that how can Xavier date me and lots of those shits.

I just moved in between them and separated them both with all the force that I can exert at that particular moment.

Xavier and Evan both were shocked as to who got the guts to separate a fighting heir of Clark family and heir of Knight family. And when they looked at me the shock was evident in their facial expressions. When I looked at Evan he didn't had much wounds that means Xavier was being civil human being and not an animal unlike my brother who was about to kill Xavier. But when I looked at Xavier I was not able to control my tears and I cried fully out loud. He have so many wounds and bruise in his body , some areas were turning purple- black . How can my brother do this to my Xavier.

I just ran towards Xavier and hugged him he also hugged me back by my waist and kept one hand at my hair. My head was placed on his chest , under his chin and I was crying. I tightly hugged him and he buried his face in my neck and gave a peck there and said.

"I am fine love . I am fine. Don't cry baby." he said But the pain was evident in his voice.

"I am sorry I am sorry. " I kept on apologizing to him.

Suddenly I remembered who did this.

I detached myself from Xavier and furiously turned around towards my brother and said.

"What the fuck is wrong with you Evan Clark. Who the hell do you think you are that you can do this to the man I love. Who the fuck you think you are. Just because you are my brother did

I signed a contract of signing my life off to you that you will take decisions for my life and I will not be able to do something for my happiness. Is that so?" I shouted at his face

"How dare you date him ella. Didn't I told you not to go anywhere near him huh?" He shouted at me.

"Just shut the fuck up ! Being my brother doesn't give you the right to control my life. My whole life you controlled me. But Xavier set me free he made me feel those emotions which nobody can let me feel. Especially you. You only know how to control me and my life. I thought when I started dating him , when you will return back i will tell you the truth and you will understand us and clear all the misunderstandings between you both but no you chose this path so let me tell you that was a wrong move ." I shouted

I can see my friends including Xavier was looking at me in shock as to I was shouting at the person whom I loved the most and I was cursing at him too. But this time I am pissed.

"I don't know what the fuck emotions you are talking about but just let me tell you , you can't date him. Lets go home we will solve this there" Evan said to me.

I just shooked my head.

The shock of disbelief was evident in his face.

"So--so you mean you choose him over me." Evan said to me

"If you can't accept our relationship, so let's face it. Yes I choose him, a thousand times over you." I said

"Are you choosing him over me ella?" Evan said with disgust all over his face.

"Till the end of my life" I said in a calm tone while holding Xaviers hand in mine.

" I am going to kill you" Evan said to Xavier .

"Over my dead body" I said and walked out from there.

I thought my life was going on smooth but after every good day a strom comes in everyone's life. And this was mine. And if Evan don't accept Xavier I am going to lose one of the most important relationship to me.

I don't know what will happen but I will hold Xavier hand till i take my last breath.

Chapter 16

Xavier

Life is so unpredictable, yesterday we were so happy to-gether, making amazing memories, I thought actually I should say i made up a plan that i will tell everything to Evan after he come back from his trip and after that I'll propose Ella for marriage but all my plans went down in vain, when that incident which happened 30 minutes ago happened.

I was practicing i didn't knew out of nowhere Evan would come and beat the shit out of Me, I could've also beaten him badly but I saw Ella face in front of my eyes and I stopped my actions of defending my self and took all the punches Evan was throwing my way . I was only seeing ella face in front of my eyes and that stabled me and my anger or else this bastard was dead today.

I don't out of nowhere ella appeared , fought with her brother and took me home. I didn't liked that she fought with her brother because I know how much he mean to her. But this time ella is really pissed and I know its better to keep quiet in this situation. Because my girlfriend looks hello angry now and i dont want her kill me if I opened my mouth unnecessarily.

Ella was driving towards my penthouse. When we reached there she helped out and we both went towards my bedroom. She gently helped me to sit on the bed And took my first kit from where she knew it was placed and started to clean my wounds.

She was only looking at my wound , not at me , she was just cleaning my wounds and all.

I gently lifted her chin to make a eye contact with her and what I saw really made my heart broke into pieces. My Ella who always was a happy girl, who can find happiness in the most smallest possibilities. Have tears in her eyes. She looked broken.

"Ella" I whispered

"I know you want to break up with me . You are this much hurt just because of me , I know but I just want to treat your wound and I will walk out of your house." she said while tears were continues to fall from the eyes I fell in love with.

"No No No baby what are you saying. Never in this lifetime I want to break up with you, what the hell made you think that." I said while wiping tears from her rosy cheeks.

She suddenly hugged me and cried on my shoulder . I kept on soothing her back while saying soothing words to her and kissing her neck .

I don't like my love crying like this. I want my ella , who only got the power to bring a genuine smile in my face . I want my ella back. Evan why you messed everything up . Because of you my ella is crying like this for the first time. I am not forgiving you for this.

"Why Xav why, why my brother did this to me . Why he hurt the person I love the most in this world. Why did he not trust me. Why did he hurt you. I loved him so much and this is what he did to me. Why Xavier Why?" She said while crying on my shoulder

I separated myself from her gently and said.

"He only did that because he loves you so much that he can't see you get hurt. You being with a guy like me made him mad. I don't deserve you I know , but I am selfish to keep you with me and that's what he is tensed about." I said to her

"How can you be this good. And why did you said you dont deserve me. I'll kill you for saying this line once you get healthy. I love you so much jerk" she said while chuckling a little

I just chuckled and said ,"I love you too my love"

We just cuddled I my bed after she treated all my wounds .We were watching Brooklyn Nine Nine when the door of my bedroom barged open revealing Zoe, Aidan , Kate and Chris. They all had worried expression on their faces.

They suddenly threw all questions at me like I am fine ,
do they need to call doctor and blah blah blah. My ella just
controlled her tears and these motherfuckers are reminding
her of the incident again.

Can't they see they are spoiling two love birds quality time .
But no they need to interrupt us. Jerks.

"I am fine guys." I said with finality in my voice.

They all nodded and sat in my bed we all started to talk but
after Zoe asked one question everything went silent.

"Ella what now?" Zoe asked.

After a good amount of five minutes ella answered

"I don't know what's gonna happen now but one thing I know
for sure is I love Xavier and I truly abide by my words and would
love to hold Xaviers hand while we go through convincing Evan
for our relationship " she said while holding my hand and
looking at it smiling.

All were looking at us with awe expression and I myself was
looking at my ella with admiration.

Don't worry ella because this Rivalry will end soon when I will
tell your brother the truth about what exactly happened in our
past.

Chapter 17

Xavier

I was getting ready for meeting Evan. It's been 3 days for now since that incident where Evan beaten the shit out of Me and since three days I was ignoring Ella.

Yes I was ignoring ella because this time I wanted to make it right. I wanted to hold her hand with all rights. I know I am making her sad . From past three days after she went home , she kept calling me and me being a jerk is not picking up her calls not even replying to her messages.

People may things it's easy for me but it's the most difficult I ever did in my whole life. This three days are the most hardest three day ever of my existence.

But , nevertheless i wanted to make it right before I made mine and ella's relationship official. I convinced Evan to come by giving him sake of ella. I asked him that if he love ella please come to our old football ground where we used to practice when we're best of Friends.

Somehow I knew he would come because I importantly mentioned that I will tell him the truth and I know in little some corner of his heart he also wants to know the truth.

So now we both are meeting in our old football club and now I am gonna tell him what is the truth of that night.

I hoped in inside my car and started to drive . When I reached there I already saw Evan car parked there . I smiled . He never changed always on time.

When I entered I was welcomed with a back facing Evan. Before I called him out he turned and shouted at me

"Firstly you are late as usual. And secondly what the fuck is the matter that you called me here so late " He shouted on me and said .

"I called you here to tell you the truth " I said

"Previously I wanted to know about truth , but after seeing your bull shit face I don't want to know about it because I know you will say lie upon lie to cover the whole truth ." he said

He said And I was walking away bit this is my last chance of making everything right.

"I was not the one who made coach let you out of the team." I said shouting a little

"What?" He shouted at me . Shock was evident in his voice.

I nodded and started the story of what really happened that day.

3 years back

EvanI was in front of the mirror fixing my hair when I got a call from my best friend Xavier. He is my best friend and I trust him the most and I know he will never hurt me.

I called him Babe because that is the name I use to tease him with .So the call was ringing with Babe name on top of it. I laugh every time he calls and he doesn't like this name too.

I picked up the call and welcomed with a loud voice of Xavier.

"I am calling you for past 15 minutes and you are not picking up my call . How the hell did you got this much guts huh?.. or are you with a girl doing inappropriate things. I swear i will kill you if I will need to solve another girl case of yours i will chop off your...." he said and I cut him of by saying.

"Babe I know you are possessive over me but no I was not with any girl . And please tell me how i got the privilege to receive a call from almighty Xavier Asher Knight" I said on a mocking tone.

"You really make me puke my guts out sometimes. Anyways we all are going to the club today and you are coming with us , I am also getting ready and I'll be there in 10 see you there tata" he said And disconnected the call without giving me a chance to talk .

Typical Xavier He will not let me talk and ask me to come somewhere but he will be the one who will be the come last to any party or occasion.

I took my car keys and drive towards our usual club.

And as usual we all were there but Xavier was late.

"Will Xavier ever get on time?" Chris said while looking at his watch.

"NOPE" Aidan replied with amusement dripping his voice and drinking his beer.

"And there our hero is what you call fashionably late." I said when xavier entered the club as usual flipping his hair once or twice in a while.

"So what we are up to guys" Xavier Said as he sat witg us and ordered a tequila for himself.

We were chatting for a while when we the most important discussion topic came up .

"I heard the tommorow coach is picking the captain of the football team and he will also finalize who all will be there in the final team of annual games of the year" Aidan said

"Yeah ! I think coach will choose Xavier as the captain . And we all will be there in the final team " Chris said

" No. I think Evan deserves to be the captain of the football team. He is good at it as well as basketball. " Xavier Said

"Oh no come on Xavier you deserve it" I said to him

"Oh shut up " he said

" will you both stop bickering let the coach choose because upto me you both deserve to be the captain" Aidan said

We were enjoying the night after that we all went towards our car and went to our separated dorms.

Xavier

I woke up with voice of my ringtone . I woke up rubbed my eyes and saw that it was chris call

"Hey man why you are calling this early in morning ?" I asked him

"Xavier just come to the football ground right now because a very big blunder occurred in here" he said in a very serious tone.

"Ok" i said And after that I started to get ready

When I reached the football field everybody is looking at me as if I done some crime.

Tyler, the only person whom I hate with every fabric of my body came and said something very absurd .

" I took your friendship . Congratulations to me on that." he said patted my shoulder and went towards parking lot.

When I looked towards football field suddenly a punch was landed on my face . I realised it was Evan, Aidan and chris tried to stop him and I also tried to defend myself but when I heard a Line coming out of Evan mouth i freezed.

" You made me out of the team . You jerk I thought you as my friend but you filled coach ears against me and showed him our chats about what I used to tell you about coach . And how I was the one who told the principal about him being too friendly with cheerleaders. How can you do that to me huh" he shouted at my face.

" what the hell are you saying , I didn't did anything like this " I said

" you just shut up you are again lying . Because of you coach threw me out of the football team and I was also not be able to be on final team. I hate you man. " he shouted and few tears escape his eyes after that he pushed me and ran towards his car.

Aidan and chis picked me up and stabled me on my two feet and just on that time near our ear Noah whispered.

"Told ya" and after realizing that Noah did this I fainted . I just heard few people shouting my name. But Evan my best friend was not one of them.

Back to the present

Xavier

"I was not the one who betrayed you , Tyler was , you were, are and always gonna be my best friend . Never ever for any-thing I will betray your trust " I said and by the time i realised we both were crying. I was crying. Yeah people I cry too.

"And let me tell you one thing I did my job of telling you the truth that it was not me it was Tyler, and if you want me to trust do it or I don't care now . Now I will be on a guilt free relationship with the person I love the most in whole world my ella . And now never try to come in between us " I said And stared to stroll out of the field where our Rivalry started and ended.

Whatever the decision of Evan might me but now I am not going to leave my ella hand ever. And that's my vow to myself.

Ella was mine and she always will be. Fuck others.

Chapter 18

Ella

It's been three days since I last met Xavier. Last three days since we talked , message or met with each other.

I just don't understand why he is ignoring me. Is he going to take off all anger of my brother anger on me. But he was the one who promised me he will make everything right . He will not leave my hand. But now he is ignoring

Yesterday Evan also went somewhere , I don't know where. I am not talking to Evan too. I am completely ignoring him . Our parents are also noticing it , but they didn't said anything about it because they also know this is something related to Me dating Xavier. Well should I say was. No Right?

But when Evan came home later late at night. He was in shock, from his face I can also see he cried and he looked in guilt. I don't know what happened but I so wanted to console my brother but with very difficultly I stopped myself.

Now I am getting ready for a new day at University. Zoe and Kate are going to pick me up because for some peculiar reasons me and Xavier are not in a very good terms.

I was just not excited to get ready today. Each day I used to get ready for Xavier but today I just don't understand why I don't want to get ready.

I just wore a beige coloured shirt and denim shorts. I didn't did any make up. Wore my sneakers , took my bag and phone and started to make my way downstairs.

I was welcomed with the sight of my family eating breakfast. I just made my way outside because I was not in the mood to eat anything.

When I went outside I waited for like five minutes and Zoe car picked me up.

In car too , I was not speaking . I think I don't have much energy to talk to anybody now.

Realizing it Zoe and kate were also quite and car atmosphere was also dense which is contradictory to the fact that there always music blasted our car. And we shouting on top of our lungs.

When we reached University, Zoe parked her car in the parking lot and we all made our way outside. I saw Xavier's car parked too. Suddenly I felt anger burned inside me.

He should be the one who should be there for me and when I needed him the most ge left hold of my hand.

When we all three entered University, every body were giving me strange looks. Some with shock, some with pity, some with disgust and some with concern and confusion.

I just made my way towards our locker because I don't have anymore energy for anymore drama in my life.

When we reached our lockers, I picked up my books and was making my ways towards my class with my friends when we saw Xavier, Aidan and Chris entering from our opposite direction.

Our eyes locked just in time and all the noise in the hallway stopped . All eyes were on us . And I knew every one were waiting for my next action.

Let Mr. Xavier Asher Knight have a taste of his own medicine.

I just made my way confidently and made my way towards classroom without acknowledging their presence.

I heard some gasp and damns . But the only voice I heard was the distinct voice of Xavier calling my name.

First three classes were amazing (note the sarcasm) . Every one showed me pity which I hated.

Now it was the most difficult time of the day. It used to be my favorite class where all six of us were together but now things are different.

I made my way towards the class and saw all five of them were sitting on our usual spot and my seat which was next to Xavier was still empty.

With a heavy heart I changed my way and sat at the distinct corner where a long window was there . I sat in that seat. I saw my friends reaction but now I don't know I just don't feel ok. I know I need Xavier but what he did to me was totally and utterly wrong. He should have atleast talked to me. But he decided to ignore me.

In middle of the class our mam excused herself to make a call and at that sudden time Xavier came and started questioning me.

"El why are you ignoring me ?" I chosed to not answer that.

And one after the other he started to throw questions at me.

I just loosed my temper and said

"Why the fuck do you care Xavier Knight? When I called you and messaged you thousands of time, you were declining my calls and leaving messages on delivered. I was just a game to you Right?. You never really loved or cared for me . Because of one fucking of your and my brothers past you left my hand . You went all M.I.A. all this past days. When I needed you the most you were not there and I am going to hate you forever for it." With that I ran towards the main gate of university.

I can't stand in that place anymore. I need place to breathe.

I sat in a cab and went towards my home. In whole journey I was crying . The cab driver gave me a tissue for which I thanked him.

When I reached my home i ran towards my room and hoped in bed.

I have no more energy. It feels like I am already dead.

I don't know when I nodded off. But I was woken up by Zoe and kate.

"What are you two doing here?" I asked them

"We know ella , whatever happened with you was very bad but now you really need to stop being this and start being your usual self . Atleast try for us" Kate said while holding my hand

I nodded with a smile because they were right.

"And you know the best way to do it is tommorow " Kate nad Zoe said

"What is tommorow?" I asked

" Come on girls don't tell me you forget tommorow is our prom day and you are coming with us. No excuses. Now get your ass up out of that bed we are going for shopping for our dress." They said

They dragged me off my bed and we started to make my way towards Zoe car.

I hope this prom will turn our life into a normal one again without any drama. A person can only wish.

Chapter 19

E lla
 Today was the day whole university was waiting for . Our prom day.

Theme was winter so everyone decided we all are going to dress in blue.

We were getting ready for the prom . We were helping each other with make up and hair too.

Our dresses were amazing.

Ella's Dress

Kate's Dress

Zoe's Dress

As we all got ready we made our way towards my car and head off towards the auditorium were prom was going to be held

When we reached there every one were so excited.

Everyone were clicking pictures. Enjoying, drinking, partying and all of that. Me , Kate and Zoe also started to enjoy ourselves. We clicked pics. They both drank and all of that.

But we suddenly stopped when our eyes locked with those certain three bad boys. Those eyes were only locked at us. I looked away from them and suddenly the stage was took by our valedictorian to gave a speech about prom. And how this year was memorable and all that. It was indeed memorable .

Let me tell you she gives amazing speeches . Her speech was so fun and up to point . After her speech we were having a talk with others.

I was completely ignoring xaviers presence but he kept on mouthing me 'sorry' or 'let's talk' and I ignored him .

Suddenly the stage was took by ... Evan?

What was Evan doing in here .and why is he standing there with a mic. All were looking at him with a confused and curious faced as to what he wanted to say. I also got very confused on what on earth he wants to say.

"I apologize for my sudden entry. I know I may spoil your prom with this speech but my confrontation is very important today " he started

" 3 years back I made the biggest mistake of my life. I misunderstood my babe, Xavier, my best friend . I thought he can hurt me or he can cheat on me. But everything was done by that person whom I was friends all this years. With one fucking misunderstanding and all are friendship went in drain . I used to trust xav with every ounce on my body and I knew he is never going to break it. But when the time came to believe him I landed punches in him without listening to his side. I turned out to be his Rival. I became such a egoistic dumb person that I didn't even understand a simple thing that Xavier can't do that to me and I also was not able to understand how much xav loves ella nobody else can"

"Yes I am saying this Xavier loves ella. And I feel so ashamed of myself that I considered and marked there love as a crime. I thought Xavier will break ella's heart but I was the one who kept on breaking my sister heart. I didn't even think about how she would be feeling when she saw the love of her life got beaten to death by her very own fucker brother. "

"But today i want to make my all mistakes right. And I will .." he said And by that time me and Xavier were crying .

He suddenly dropped the mic and started to make way towards me. He came and stood in front of me , took hold of my hand started to drag me towards Xavier. I got confused what's happening

And suddenly when we reached there he took Xavier hand and placed my hand on top of it , smiled and made his way out.

But he stopped and turned around and said " he is not anymore your brothers Rival ella .. he was and is your brothers best friend and xav Your ella is now yours nobody is going to take her away from you." he said And made his way far from us and stand next to Chris and Aidan.

I looked at Xavier and we both have the same expression on our faces we were crying and laughing at the same time and suddenly he landed his lips on mine. This is what I was waiting for my whole life.

Xavier

She is the missing puzzle of my life, she is my everything. After we broke the kiss we hugged. We hugged wach other so much tightly that we both will dissappear into thin air.

Everybody were hooting and clapping at us but our both concentration were in each other

"Best day of my life." She whispered into his ear and he responded

"Same here love. I got my everything back " he said

We broke the hug , we rested our foreheads on each other's and were giggling . It was a magical moment. I wanted it to last forever.

"I love you my sunshine, my love , my everything " he said

"Thank you for dripping all your coffee at Me and I am in debt of Aidan forever that he took me there where I met you" he said while laughing

" I love you my bad boy forever and ever in this lifetime " I said And landed my lips on his.

I didn't knew my senior year was going to be this Normal (sarcasm) .

But I couldn't ask for anything better. Not now not anymore. I got what I wanted. What I needed. My bad boy. My Xavier.

Epilogue

----

3 years Later

Ella

"Can you please pass the hair spray dear" my hair dresser asked me while my make up artist was doing something to my face.

My brides maid that were Emma, Kate and Zoe were already ready in their beautiful bridesmaid gown . Everything was just perfect.

And if u still hadn't got the idea what is today then let me announce that today is the union ceremony or in normal human language of mine and Xavier.

I am so excited , oh god literally I can't stop bouncing and all. But controlling u know...

I got ready in my beautiful wedding dress and it was .... damn

I am so happy . I am having mixed emotions today I can't believe from today from Ella Clark I'll be Ella Knight .

I got ready and of course my mom , dad , brother and Olivia got emotional by seeing me and don't get be Staarted on my bridesmaid.

I got into the car and we started to make way towards our wedding venue.

I wanted to keep everything simple . But Knights.

We reached there and the decor there was so beautiful. Everything was a dream come true.

Wedding planner told me to enter when music starts playing and in less than 2 minutes music started playing

Oh my God he remembers 'A thousand years' started playing and from that moment I was in tears. I feel so lucky and blessed that I am marrying such a man who loves and respect me so much.

I entered and there he was the love of my life my Xavier, standing there at the altar as he promised in his black tux looking so glorious. He have teras in his eyes and I know he must be biting his tounge to control it.

Aidan and chris were standing next to him still being idiots showing me thumbs up and some biceps move or something. Idiots are still idiots after 3 years.

I reached at the altar and my father gave my hand to my forever partner.

"You look beautiful " he whispered

I couldn't help but blush at that moment which led him to have his famous smirk.

"Today we have gathered here for the holy matrimonial union of Mr. Xavier Knight and Ms. Ella Clark , Please Repeat after me." Priest said to me and Xavied and then started our wedding vows."You are my person, my inspiration, my love and my everything. I cannot wait to spend a lifetime loving you."

"I vow to express my love for you as often as I breathe each breath."

"You are the person I want to spend forever with."

"As I have spent my whole life looking for my other half, I knew it was you from the moment we met."

"Although it is until death do us part, I know that we will never truly part because our souls are made for each other.I promise that each kiss will be filled with more love than the last and that our days together will grow in love and devotion. From today onward, you and I will be one in heart, body and mind.I vow to cherish you, devote my life to you and always be true. Let us build a home, a life and a family from our bonds of true love and our vows to stick together through all life's challenges."

" Do you Xavier Knight take Ella Clark as you lawfully wedded wife to have and to hold , to better or worst, in rich or poorer , in sickness and in health and as long as you both shall live"

"I do" He said with so much love in his voice without any hesitation.

" Do you Ella Clark take Xavier Knight as you lawfully wedded husband to have and to hold , to better or worst, in rich or poorer , in sickness and in health and as long as you both shall live"

"I do" I said And that's were everything became forever.

We both exchanged rings and...

"With the power vested in me I pronounce you man and wife , you may kiss your wife"Priest said and walked away

"Congratulations Mrs. Knight" He said And kissed the life out of me , it was such a kiss that our whole life depended on it in that situation.

We broke our kiss and rested our foreheads against each other

"Congratulations to you to hubby." I said while smiling.

He smiled and said "thank you for spilling coffee on me love"

I laughed and said "Thank god I spilled it."